Searching for North.

At the back of the house by the old stables, Amelia watched North, the young man her husband Aubrey had brought down from London to be footman and chauffeur, wash down the car. Must you go? she had asked, and knew as the words left her lips, that of course he must. He spoke of duty to King and Country, and she nodded. Aubrey had enlisted the young man into his own regiment. Not to be without him, he had said. But what of her? she had mused silently, watching the strong hands and arms move over the car. He called her Madam. Spoke softly. She sighed. He held his head to one side like a bird looking for worms. She smiled as she walked around him as he worked. Madam sounded so distant. Amelia she had said, call me Amelia. And he had, the few times, alone together; had held her and she melted as if her body were ice left in the sun.

She remembered his hand in hers. Felt it again as she sat in the dining room at breakfast. Aubrey's letter on the table in front of her, dated that fateful year 1916. North lost to us. The word us touched her. She wondered if Aubrey knew he'd been cuckolded. Her eyes were full. She gazed at the room; at Aubrey's ancestors looking down at her from their stiff frames. Nell, the maid stood by the window, her small hands tucked inside each other, gazing out at the cold morning. Amelia wished she were one she could express her grief to, but she was too young; a gossip she expected. What could she say? Whom could she ever tell? She felt the tears brimming up in her eyes. The room became watered and blurry. She lifted a spoon to her lips, but stopped as if she never wanted to eat again; never wanted food or drink to pass her lips again. Suddenly, the sobs broke from her, as if an enormous eruption of grief could be contained no longer, and broke free from her in such a way that the maid stood and stared as if her mistress had broken into a brief, but deep madness. Amelia stuffed her napkin to her mouth to hold back the eruption; her hands acting like headless chickens, moving wildly. Nell, after a few seconds of hesitation, ran to her mistress; stood awkwardly, gaping, unsure whether to hold or touch or run for help, but broke from her restraint; embraced Amelia as if she were a child who had been badly hurt. Amelia sensed the embrace; wanted to sink deeper and deeper; to lose herself in the small arms and stiff breast. Her sobs broke out. Her hands held close the body of the maid as if to a lover, as if it were North himself had come back to her. Nathan North, Nathan. The name in her head rang out like a bell. Nell looked down at the hair and head against her; felt her own tears welling up. She mumbled words, but they were lost amongst the waves of grief; tossed aside as so much flotsam on the waters of this broken heart and soul. Calmed, Amelia lifted her head, dabbed her eyes, smiled weakly at Nell, held one of the small hands, looked at it, held it briefly against her cheek. Bad news, she muttered. The War. Deaths always deaths. The Master had written. North had been killed. Nell sensing nothing of deeper grief, bit her lip; stared at Amelia, pushed her free hand to her mouth; let tears fall. Later Amelia stood at the window of her bedroom and stared at the moon in the night sky. Nathan North was out there cold in the night air. His hands and arms still now. She sighed. Aubrey spoke of other things in his letter, but they were as nothing to her. She moved her finger along the glass pane as if to write the name there; to write all that she felt and suffered. Nell stood beside her in silence. Words seemed wasted. What were words worth now? Amelia thought, sensing the maid at her side, smelling the scent of soap; the scent of flowers. She wondered what the girl made of it all; what she thought about the tears shed; the moodiness; the refusal of food; the deep sighs. She wondered how Nathan had died, how he had met his end. Had it been sudden? She mused, biting her lower lip, letting her hand fall from the windowpane and rest by her side, touching briefly that of the maid. Tomorrow she would go to the stables, stare at the car; see if North was there. Maybe it was a mistake. she told herself, maybe Aubrey had got it wrong, had named another. She had the letter in the pocket of the dress she had worn that morning. How cold ink seemed, how indifferent to the message written. Nell spoke. Words. Soft words. Words that hung in the air like cigarette smoke. Amelia shook her head. Stay, she had muttered. She wanted the girl to stay. Not leave now. She asked; did not order; looked away from the window; gazed at the maid; gazed like onc wounded. The girl nodded. If Nathan were here, would he have nodded, too? she wondered, smiling sadly, touching the girl's small hand. Stay. Nodded. How to heal such pain, how to comfort such grief, none knew. Nell drew the curtains as if the show had ended; moved to turn down the bed; waited like one in the wings for the next act to begin, for the next change of scenery, the learned lines to be forgotten. All was set. The lamp was dampened. Darkness embraced them. And out in some cold field on foreign soil North lay spoiled and lone, as far off two bodies embraced searching for him in their grief held sleep.

Never Go Away.

And there was that small room with a bathroom attached just off Trafalgar Square said Netanya and it had been booked by Benedict to go to after the show in a theatre near Victoria Station and my husband at that time said Where are you going? and I said To London to see a show and What time will you be back? Sunday afternoon I said You're staying over night? he said Yes I said Who are you going with? he asked That's my business I said and anyway when the Saturday came for me to go I met Benedict at the station he had been waiting anxiously in case I couldn't get away and I had a small overnight bag with my change of clothes in and wash stuff and he had a duffel bag and I said Well here I am and he said Wasn't sure you'd get away and I said Well he was suspicious but that's his problem and we got on the train to London and it was our first time together away from our local sites and he was looking at me and I think he was conscious for the first time of our age differences I was his senior by thirteen years and it didn't seemed to show in our own town but now out of the area it did seem to show a bit but I put it out of my head and hoped I was up to the challenge not having regular sex for some time and my husband at that time wasn't up to much at least not with me- he had had sex with anyone else between sixteen to sixty- but me no it was sparse and anyway I was glad at the time thinking I didn't want to catch anything he may have caught from some slag- and we sat and talked and Benedict talked of Sartre and Camus but I didn't know who they were so just pretended I did and about existentialism and such words he went on about but it was him I watched not his words they swept over me like water in the sea and I was glad we were away and I thought briefly what the kids might be doing with me not around over the next day but they'd cope after all a woman has to live her life when she can and what chance would I have again and I recalled the first time I met Benedict and he was introduced to me at the workplace and I thought to myself he's a bit of all right and he smiled and I was kind of blown away but I knew he was having it off with another who had no luggage with her but then that blew away and I thought now is my chance and this was it and once the train entered Victoria Station and we got out and it seemed like a whole new world with so many people and we were just two people in a sea of humanity and we saw the show at the time it said and sat and watched the show and I was aware of him beside me and thought about afterwards at the room he had booked and what it would be like and would I be able to perform after all it wasn't as though I had sex often and apart from my then husband and a boy back in the early 1950s I was not quite that experienced at sex or so I thought much as I liked what I had had but Benedict was younger and seemed quite a one with the girls and I thought it maybe a big let down and I'd be shown to be just a woman in her middle age crisis stage but after the show which was quite good we got a taxi to the address Benedict had shown the driver and in no time we were there and we got in the door and the woman looked at us as we booked in and I thought she looked at me with a stern eye but we didn't care she showed us the room and left us to it shutting the door behind us and telling us if we wanted the gas fire on we would need to put 50p in the meter each time it went out so I found a 50p coin and put it in the slot and turned on the gas fire and it roared into life and we looked around the room and I looked into the bathroom and it had a big deep bath and I thought that will come in handy later and I showed Benedict and he said We can bath together and I thought I have never bathed with anyone else before and he said There's always a first time for everything then we looked at the bed and sat on it and bounced on it and it seemed all right if a little bit hard but it would do us Benedict said So what now? he said and I said Well why waste time and began to undress first by taking off my coat and then my cardigan and he watched at first uncertain and I thought he's been put off about this after all and I got as far as my blouse when he took off his jacket and I watched him and he took off his tie and then we both seemed to race the other to undress first and it was like being a teenager again rather than a forty year old woman with a thirteen year younger man and I was right down to my underwear and bra and he was completely bare and stood there and then climbed into bed and waited for me and I took off what else I had on and we were both in bed naked and it was so strange so surreal and I couldn’t believe I was actually there with him and he lay there beside me looking at me and he switched off the bedside lamp and we were in the semi-dark except for the flashing on and off of neon lights and street light outside in the street and then he kissed me and his hands were on my thighs and I was unsure if I was doing the right thing but then I thought O to hell with it and kissed him more and we going at it quite strong and I didn't realise how much I never knew and how much I enjoyed what I was learning and once we had done we lay back and I looked at the room and felt him beside me and breathed in the air and him and my scent and the sounds of London out there and after that we were at it again and again until it seemed we were never going to stop and then we bathed together and I felt so young again and then we slept and had sex and bathed again and then it was morning and we left the room and the woman looked at us and I winked at her and she looked away and it was a day that day never to go from my mind never go go away.

The Sad Stare.

Christina screws up the piece of paper and throws it in the waste bin by her bed. She wants to write a love letter, but it won't come out right, the words come out wrong. She sits on her bed sucking the end of the pen. At school she can think of lots of things she wants to say to him, but putting it into a letter is different. The words look weak; seem unable to carry what she wants to say. She has got as far as, Dear Benedict, three times and after that it goes all wrong; either she says too much too soon or she struggles to get the words in the right place. She sits staring at the blank paper, pen in mouth, sucking. Her mother was in one of her moods when she got in from school; it was always something that was wrong with how she left her bedroom, leaving clothes on the floor, not putting clean clothes away, leaving hairs in the sink, or the tooth powder tin lid was left off. She stomped up stairs while her mother was calling out to her not to leave her underclothes under the bed. She had slammed the door to shut words off from her hearing. When I was a girl I'd have had my backside slapped for acting like you do to me, her mother had moaned. She leaned against the door with her body pressed against it, her hand's palms flat against the wood panels. Now she sits wanting to write to Benedict. Love letter. Letter of love. She closes her eyes and imagines he's there in her room. Beside her on the bed, looking over her shoulder, chin maybe resting on her shoulder.

She sighs softly. Then what? Downstairs her mother has switched on the radio and it is on loud, sweeping up the staircase along the passage to her room. She wouldn't mind if it was something she liked, but it was classical stuff, highbrow music, her brother calls it. Her mother says it soothes her nerves, allows her to unwind, forget the day's worries and concerns. She opens her eyes and stares at her reflection in the dressing table mirror. She wishes she had wavy or curly hair, not straight and hanging there like dull brown curtains. Her nose is stubby, her mouth shapeless. She purses her lips and makes a kissing sound. She puts down the pen and puts the paper and pen on the bed. She gets up and stands in front of the mirror. She embraces herself. Turning around and looking over her shoulder it appears as if she is being embraced by another. She moves her hands up and down her back. Imagines it is Benedict embracing her. Funny to look at. What if he could see her now? Sad cow, he'd think, embracing herself in front of a mirror. But he isn't there, she's alone, looking at her reflection, embracing, mouthing words. At school the other day, on the sports field, during lunch recess, he had come along to her and she left her group of friends, and walked off with him up the field. She held his hand. Felt the warmth of it, the flesh on flesh thing. She even moved her fingers to feel his more closer. They had talked as they walked, he about his passion for art or how he wanted to write one day and have a popular novel done, she talked about her mother's moods, the rows, the threatened good hidings, the misunderstandings, her big brother and things, but she said nothing more on that, some things were best left unsaid. They had walked to the far fence of the school grounds and stared at the passing traffic. They were near to the small woodlands by the sports field. She'd heard of at least two girls going in there with boys and doing things. She didn't know much more, probably gossip anyway, she had thought, standing next to him by the fence. She wanted to kiss him, but he didn't want to, she thought, because others might see. They stood there talking, then silence, holding hands. As they walked back down the field she wanted to rush back to the woodland with him and at least kiss him. But they walked on down the field towards the playing area, where the playground for the boys was one side of the school, and the playground for the girls the other side. Once hidden by the wall he kissed her. Quickly, suddenly, lips touching, pressing, then apart and off he went and she walked on, all built up inside with whatever it was bubbling inside. She does another turn in front of her mirror, still embracing. If only it was him, not her arms or hands, but his. Smoothing her hair, holding her close, fingers touching along her spine. One hand reaching to touch a buttock. She shuts her eyes. Seems more better to imagine him being there, doing those things. The other night in bed she put his photograph(which he had given her after she had given him one of her) next to her heart and held it there, well it was pressed against her left breast, but it was the closest she could get. Then she had kissed it over and over and put it under pillow and slept all night dreaming of him. She sighs. Looks at herself, the reflection, the straight dull hair, grey cardigan and green skirt, white socks. The music is still loud downstairs, her mother is singing what she says is an aria or some such thing. She prefers the music she hears on the small radio under her bed covers and blankets, some foreign radio station, pop music, singing about love and kisses, and boys and lovers. Soon be time for dinner. Her mother will call up and say DINNER IS ON THE TABLE, loudly, desperately, as if her all day has been for that one moment. Best get out of my school clothes, she muses, or she'll moan about that, too. She takes off the cardigan and throws it on the back of a chair by her bed. She undoes the green tie and throws it aside. She unbuttons the white blouse slowly, thinking how good it would be if Benedict was there to do it. DINNER IS READY her mother calls, the words overriding the music, the words heavy as lead. OK, COMING, she bellows back. She throws the blouse and skirt on the floor and grabbing jeans and pink top she hurriedly dresses, then gazing at her reflection once more in the mirror, she licks a finger and runs it over her eyebrows. On the bed, pen and paper lie unused. She looks at them there. Maybe after dinner she will try again. If Benedict was there she could tell him, could show him, could hold him, squeeze him to her. But he was miles and miles away in his own small village, she is here, alone, unembraced, unkissed, wanting him, needing him, wishing for him to be there, but he isn't, just her gazing at the mirror at herself standing giving her the sad stare.

Farewell to Maggie.

The steam train was about to pull out from the station; I looked at Maggie; I thought to myself, I can't let her go just like this and not say a word, or at least give her a hint how much I love and feel about her; how the mere sight of her eyes and her smile drives me crazy; that dark hair of hers that touches her shoulders and hangs there so that I want to sense its softness; smell the shampoo and scent of her; how I dream of her and want her near and close. I thought of the last few days we'd been together; the hours we'd shared; that now it was about to end as soon as the dammed train pulled out. So I took her hand through the train window; kissed it; I didn't give a monkey's pee what the other people in the compartment thought, I just wanted to say the words inside me, the words that now seemed to be hiding from me in the far away corridors of my mind. I struggled for words; looked at her as the train started to move; I began to run with the train along the platform slowly; I could see tears in her lush blue eyes; I let her hand go as my breath began to fail; I stood watching her hand and her face disappear from me; the words came soft and slow; they hung about me like reluctant hounds; the train was gone; so was Maggie; the horizon was blank and empty like my day and the days and years to come.

The Other Side of Life.

Breakfast each morning is always the same with Edward reading his newspaper and you sitting opposite dressed up and wanting him to speak and engaged you in conversation but he doesn't he just reads and takes bites of toast or sips of coffee and even when Ellie the maid lingers looking at you or putting down a coffee-pot or removing a plate you know she’s eager to say something to you but she doesn’t she just goes off in her soft footed way her black and white uniform clean and neat and her hair done nicely and as you look over at Edward his eyes still glued to the paper you wish to hell he’d just go off to the office (and his secretary whom you know he’s shafting whenever he gets the chance) so that you can begin your own day and after Ellie has done with her immediate tasks and seen Edward go off down the drive to the road his hat and coat on his briefcase in his hand you two are then alone and can give that first hold and kiss of the day and make quick plans where you can go and what to see or what you can do like yesterday's trip to the zoo but at the moment he’s still sitting there stiff and clean and mind full of stocks and shares and the money markets and the latest news from a cold world and no doubt think about the secretary bitch and you become fidgety and in between sip of coffee or nibbles of toast glance over at him or at Ellie if she enters the room again with a tray or refill of toast or bread and she looks at you and you can see in her eyes that same impatience for him to be gone and the day to begin and you gaze at her hands the nimble fingers the nails manicured by you the skin red from the washing water but which you rub with oils when you can and as she turns you look at her narrow waist how you love you wrap your arms about her and kiss her and feel her lips on yours and at the back of your mind that fear that one day he'll come home unexpectedly and see you kissing her or find you in bed with her beneath the covers snuggling up close kissing and making love as only she knows how and you remember the first time how frightened you were and so innocent of how and what to do and yet so wanting to and needing to and even now as you sit and stare at Edward's newspaper at his fingers holding it you can still recall that first time and not even Edward's sexual advances in the nightly bed and his entering you can make one iota of difference to how you feel about Ellie and the lovemaking and even at Edward's peak when he's well on his way to spurting his semen inside you all you can think on is Ellie and her way with your body compared with his and when he reaches that moment and is all yes yes yes you pretend it's Ellie there her hair against your cheek her lips kissing and as you think on this Edward lowers his paper and says Oh I'm out tonight got a meeting with DH and will stay at my club afterwards and I may be late home tomorrow so don't wait up for me and you say Ok Edward hope your meeting goes well and you know he's going to be shagging the secretary full on and as Ellie enters the room her eyes bright her hands rubbing together and you both smile at the thought of another night.

An April In Paris.

Always do what Miss Maxell tells you, Milly, your mother had said when you went to live in and work as a maid at the big house outside the small town. But even your mother would never have understood where that had led and as you sit with Miss Maxell outside a café in Paris, musing on your mother's words and taking in the sights and sounds around you, a thrill of excitement flows through your veins. Even the clothes you wear you could never have afforded on your wages, from the hat she brought you down to the stockings on your feet inside the shoes. The underwear are so smooth, so soft and so expensive. Just like hers. You'd seen them, washed them, felt the texture of them. Now you wore some the same. You look around you. Paris. You can hardly believe you are actually here. When she said she was going to bring you to Paris you thought it was just an empty promise, a kind of bribe for sleeping with her. But no, you are actually here. The sights. The smells. The sounds. Let me do the talking, Miss

Maxell had said. She spoke French; you didn't. And when you hear her speaking to the waiter, you have to look at her because she seems like another, as if some other young woman had sat beside you and taken Miss Maxell's place. Call me Millicent, she had told you. Miss Maxell sounds too formal and will give the game away if you are heard, she had told you in bed the night before you had left for Paris. Saying her name, saying Millicent, sounds odd. It sticks in your throat like a fish bone. Millicent, Millicent, you utter silently to yourself as Millicent orders the drinks and turns to you after the waiter has gone and smiles one of her smiles, and her hand touches yours on the table. Just for a few moments. The feel of it. Hers on yours. Here in Paris. Mother would not have understood this. Even when you lay in bed with Millicent in the night and you and she make love and you following her directions and sensing things you had never sensed before, you think of your mother and what she would have said had she seen all that and overheard the conversations. Poor Mother would have rolled over and died. Funny things, Mother's words. Always do what Miss Maxell tells you, Milly. You did. You do. And here you are outside the café in Paris; you and Millicent and no one knows. No one here knows or cares or gives you a second look. No one. The waiter comes with the coffee and you sip it as Millicent has shown you. You have never tasted coffee like this. The sensation sits on your tongue. The taste buds are alive and want more. Millicent sips hers. You watch her hand holding the cup, the fingers, the way her mouth opens, the lifting of the cup, the lips touching, the swallow. The fact that you are here watching her seems so surreal, as if you are dreaming it all and will wake up and find yourself lying in bed looking up at the off-white ceiling of your small attic room at the big house. No, you are in Paris. Here now. The sight of her beside you sipping, her eyes on you, she smiling and you smiling back, wondering where all this will lead you and where it could go, and as you sip the coffee you remember the first time she had you in her bed, and you so innocent, so unsure, and how she had taken you through the various sensations and feelings, and her soft voice there gently guiding and uttering words as if they were butter, as if you were melting in her arms and she in yours, and the utter thrill of each touch, and the sensations flowing through each nerve of your body, brought you suddenly alive, as if you had been dead and now were brought into being, like being reborn, and she kissing you and holding you, and you returning those kisses and embraces with equal passion and need, and now as she offers you a cigarette and you place it between your lips and she lights it with her silver cigarette lighter, you want to make love to her again and again, and she whispers those words leaning over the small table outside the café in Paris, and her eyes have that tint of blue in which you can see reflected two young women and they are you, dressed and looking just like you, and it is you, and you are alive and feeling and sensing, and the old you, the maid, the girl from the small town, seems far away, seems to be some other, some one you once knew, gradually leaving, waving, turning away and then Millicent sitting there, her lips parted, the smile, the gaze, the hands holding the coffee cup, the hat, the clothes, the woman, you and she and no one the wiser, no odd looks, no comments. Just the beginning, Millicent says, tapping your hand, the skin on skin, the words filling you, entering you, and all is new and fresh and reborn, and neither the waiter rushing around nor the other people around you sitting, talking, eating and drinking seem so alive, but half dead or dying, and you smile at her, Miss Maxell, Millicent, expecting nothing, wanting nothing more, than just this, this now, this moment, this being so alive, so utterly here, and Millicent saying near to you, I love you Milly, I love you, my dear.

Love & Marriage.

Marriage was a fine institution your father said but not when you were married to Clifton it wasn't not when you had him breathing all over you every time he caught you lying down trying to plant a kiss on your lips or brow or where ever he could plant one and even when he was dressed for work at the office he'd sneak a quick kiss on you or want a promise that when he got home that night you'd be waiting for him in that nightdress he bought the one with the small flowers on it the one that came just above the knees and off he'd go with that smile on him that look in his eyes that sexy brooding kind of look that I can't wait until tonight sort of gaze but once he was gone and you were sure he'd not be back for a few hours you quickly washed and dressed and went to Max's place and he'd let you in and pour you a drink and light you a cigarette and together you'd plan what you'd do for the day and where you'd go and while he dressed you talked to him through the door of the bathroom looking around his small apartment and the unmade bed and the drawn curtains and the few pictures on the walls and the one photo by the bed a photo he kept of you the one you'd given him after you first met him that night at the jazz club where Clifton had taken you and while Clifton was talking to the trumpet player in the interval the tenor sax player gave you a wink and that was Max and he came down and sat beside you and talked and talked and made you laugh and feel good for the first time in ages and all the while Clifton was with the trumpet player paying you no attention at all not even when he looked over and saw you and Max sitting together laughing and joking and since that night you and Max met whenever you could and sometimes you went out places and saw the sights and had a meal and a few drinks or you'd stay at his place and go to bed and have sex while jazz played on the radio and Max would be kissing your lobes or your lips and all you wanted was for it not to end although you knew it had to and you had to go back home to Clifton and be ready for him and his ways and wants and his kinky sex deeds and then and only then did he want his dinner want the meal hot and ready and a glass of his favourite beer and all the time asking you what you did all day and why was the place such a shambles and didn't you do any housework and you'd sit there watching him answering him monosyllabically all the while thinking of Max and the places you'd been the laughs you had had the love making in his bed the sheets the pillows the scent of him and sometimes when Clifton was beside you in the bed in your mind it was Max there Max's arms about you and his kisses on your lips and cheeks and only the dull moans of your dull husband broke the illusion of a great night's passion.

Promises Promises.

Ciara opens the curtains and peers out at the new day. The sun's weak, not much heat there. Feels the chill on skin. Rubs the arms with hands, notices Whelan in the garden, the spade thrusting in and out of the soil. Fingers beneath the armpits, feels the hairs there, rough, like tobacco, like the shag her da smoked. His calloused hands, the fingers stuffing tobacco between papers or into the pipe's bowl. Lifts her fingers to her nose. Sniffs. Odour. Need to bath. Didn't last night. Couldn't be bothered to get the tin bath down from the back wall and fill with water from the kettle. Too long. Kettle after kettle. Standing there waiting watching the steam rise, the chill from the room biting the flesh. And Whelan groping, the hands around the waist, the tongue at the neck licking. Filthy tongue; don't know where it's been. Gave up on her and went to bed with his tail between his legs. She watches from the window as Whelan bends to pick at the soil, his backside broad as a bull's, his cap back of his head, cigarette stuck behind the ear for later. She scratches her behind. The itch. The scratch. The relief. Looks back at the bed. Unmade. As it was an hour since. Musky. Sheets everywhere. Human smell. His dirty clothes on the floor, cast off, lay where they were thrown. She picks up the cigarette packet, takes out a cigarette, and puts between the lips. Paper on skin. Sticks there. She takes out a match from the box and lights the cigarette. Inhales. Puffs. Hits the throat, the lungs. The taste. First of the day. Deep inhalation.

Satisfaction. Exhales. Smoke rises. Da made rings with smoke. Fascination as a child. Watching. Seeing the smoke rise. Ring after ring. Da sitting there smiling at my joy of watching. Memories. Many of them. The yellow between fingers, the burn marks. Ciara stands and watches Whelan dig once more. The spade thrust deep, the thighs strong, the hands pushing down, the arms strong. Just the once, he asked the night before. Too tied. Need my sleep. That had him. Put his penis away like a spoilt child. Moans, groans, sighs. Can't always be bothered with the sex. All effort no result. No child. Nothing. Barren. She watches the cap on the back of his head rise and fall with the thrust of him. The cigarette still there behind the ear. The promise made to him. If you're good maybe. Early to bed early to rise. She remembers Kenny, her first love, his exploits, his favours, his lust, hers, together. Marvellous. Couldn't get enough. Never enough. His tongue, his penis, him, her, love, lust. Then the bullet in the head; dead in some ditch. Retaliation killing. Being Catholic. One for one. Just that. Saw him that last time. Remembers that. Whelan away on business. The bed never shook so. The sex hot as hell. Remembers. Whelan stands erect, rubs his back. Looks up at her standing at the window and waves at her. Second best. Him between the sheets. Nothing like. Kenny like the Dodo: extinct. Gone, no more. She inhales. The smoke hits the back of thc throat. Fills the lungs. She scratches the cheek of the behind. The itch. The scratch. She smiles at Whelan. Sees his face relax. The muscles ease. The eyes light up. Promises promises promises. Pretend games. Make it more interesting. He likes that. He turns away, spade held, then thrust into the soil again. The weather is changing. The sky's dim. Here comes the wetness, here comes the rain.

Passions of Paris.

We seek the streets of Paris, said Claudette, the lights and sights whirl our minds and souls. Albertine clings to my arm, her words in my ears, her tongue promising things that the dark holds and kindles. We lounge in the cafés and bars; drink the wines and coffees; eat the meals with our finicky fingers; make love in the bed of the Passion d'hôtel. Men chat us up, seek our favours, want to deflower; the nights are our fields, the streets our paradise; the men leave us to our lone walks, our wanton ways. My papa would saunter the streets like a lost soul; his half-sighted eyes would bruise my mama's flesh with the tainted touch, with the loose words, the poxed penis. My mama held her séances in the back room with the curtains drawn; the long dead would speak in the ears; the knocking wood, the moving glass would bring her brother to her side from his muddy trench, where he was blown dead and wide. Albertine loves Monet: the art, the colours, the beauty of the paint; her finger runs the course of brush marks, on the art, the line of figures, the shape of colour with her eyes. I kiss her lips with the heat of passion; l hold her close as a shadow's shape; I seek her dark spaces, her sexy depths. The Sacre Coeur is our nightly haunt; our childhood God lingers in each cold stone and coloured glass; the Mass and the Crucified feed our lostness; our salvation seeping. Her brother sought her bed and spoiled her childhood; her papa drank the nights like a dark sponge; her mama in her moody darks, beat her with the cooking spoon or the copper stick. Albertine stands by the window and counts the stars; the moon mocks her with its cheesy smile; the city's lights sing to her mind and soul. We are the sisters of the streets; our wanderings are noticed by the wanton men; the theatres, the opera, the gardens, the playgrounds of our lusts and love. We know the secrets of the flesh; know the passions of our lust; we lie abed gazing at each other in each other's eyes, brushing away the hair from eyes; running a finger along the skin; tongue on tongue; sense the bed's cloth on naked backs, the warmth, the heat; the kisses touch; the finger's feel; the whispered words. My papa's grave is crowded with weeds, the stone fading, his name almost lost; my mama sits deranged in an asylum bed, her world spinning away from our common sphere. Albertine loves the arts; the artist's realm; the smell of paint, the touch of oils on her skin. She licks my ear in her passion's drive; her tongue wanders my flesh, wets my sex to the heights of heaven and hell. We walk arm in arm, hand in hand, the tut-tutting follows us as we pass, the curses touch the hems of dresses, the pointed words sharpen on our skins. We sip the wines on street cafés; drench ourselves in our nightly baths, drown our bodies in each other's passion and love our crucified god in our own lost fashion.

Lily Lavatera.

Lily Lavatera placed her pen down on the desk. The letters can wait, she said to herself, staring momentarily at the photograph of Edward Wynsor propped on her desk in front of her. Studying the black and white photograph, she sensed her eyes fill with tears.

News of Edward's death the day before had almost undone her; it came in a letter from one of his closest friends, with whom he served with the regiment in Libya. What was worse, Edward's wife, Alisma, would also be grieving at this moment in time, unaware, Lily hoped, that she had been Edward's lover. And what was worse, Lily and Alisma were close friends, although they had not seen each other for some time. For a few moments the photograph became blurred as tears filled her eyes, but she wiped her eyes with her right hand and looked away from the celluloid image.

Getting up from the desk she walked to the fireplace and stood for a few minutes staring into the flames. Then she pushed the bell on the wall and waited for the maid. Standing by the fireplace, she could see out of the large window that revealed the cold February morning. She shuddered. The thought of Edward no longer walking with her out across the lawn, between the groves of elms, filled her with a deep dread, and threatened to fill her eyes with tears again.

- You rang, Miss? the young maid asked, entering the room.

-Yes, Daisy. Could you bring me some tea? Lily said without turning round.

- Yes, Miss, Daisy Chayne said, curtsying out of the room, even though her mistress hadn't turned round.

The door eased shut behind her. Lily went to the window and peered out on to the frost-ridden lawn. All seemed to be blanketed with a thin whiteness which hardened and sometimes killed. Moving her eyes across the lawn, she let them fall on the far summerhouse where she and Edward frequently went to be alone on late summer evenings. Her mind at that moment drifted back to the previous year, just prior to Christmas, when he came and stayed a few days before returning to his wife and son George home from boarding school. They had gone to the summerhouse, though it was winter, to escape the cold breeze.

- It’s been quite a year, Edward said. Battle of Britain and all that, and us too much apart.

- Yes, too much apart, Lily had said and mouthed the words now looking out at the far summerhouse frosted up. And that had been the last time they had made love. Up in her bedroom when all others were asleep and Edward had crept surreptitiously along the passageway to find her. Yet, she mused to herself sadly, I didn't feel any sense of guilt. Never for a moment thought about Alisma. Until now. The door opened slowly and Daisy entered holding a tray with teapot, cup and saucer, milk jug and sugar bowl and placed them cautiously on the small table by the fireplace.

- Will there be anything else, Miss? Daisy asked. Lily turned from the window and gazed at her maid for a few seconds.

- What did you think of Major Wynsor, Daisy? Lily enquired in a low voice. Daisy bit her lower lip for a few moments in what passed for thought, and scratched her chin to give the impression of deep consideration.

- Well, he was always nice to me, Miss, Daisy replied quietly.

- Yes, Lily said, but what did you think of him as a person?

Daisy stiffened and bit her lip again. Her eyes lowered to the carpet. - Very brave, Daisy ventured. I mean, him being out there fighting the Germans and away from his family and all that. Daisy dried up. She lifted her eyes to her mistress. I expect his wife will grieve for him something rotten, Daisy added as an afterthought. And you too, of course, Miss, she further added, moving her face into an attempted smile.

Lily nodded, but did not reply straight away, but instead turned once again to scan the lawn for Edward. Lily could hear Daisy moving uneasily behind her, waiting to be dismissed.

- Daisy, sit down for a moment, she said. She heard the maid plonk herself noisily in one of the armchairs by the fireplace. The girl was a terrible fidget, Lily mused, wishing she could see Edward, but knowing she wouldn't.

Finally, after a minute staring at the lawn without Edward, she turned and sat in the armchair opposite Daisy.

-We need another cup, Lily said gently.

- Who for, Miss? Daisy asked dimly.

- You, Lily said, nodding towards her maid. Daisy blushed.

- Me, Miss? Oh, I couldn't. What would Cook say? Daisy uttered.

- Leave Mrs Coix to me and get another cup, Lily stated firmly. Daisy stood, curtsied and left the room like the timid mouse she seemed. Lily smiled. Poor girl, she mused, a bag of nerves. No wonder, I suppose, with Mrs Coix in charge of her, Lily mused, smiling briefly. Looking across at the armchair opposite, she remembered that Edward loved to sit there, and gaze out at the view of the lawn and the distant summerhouse. And for a few moments she thought she could see him there, smiling in that way he had, gazing at her profoundly has he always did with those deep blue eyes of his. Wonder what he'd say about inviting the maid to drink tea with me? Lily mused darkly. Frown on it no doubt. Got to keep them in their place, Lily, he'd say, when she seemed too kind or considerate to him with servants. But today was different. She wanted someone who knew her and Edward, to open up and say what they thought or knew. She was sure Daisy would open up. Did Daisy know about her and Edward? she asked herself. Know about us making love in my room at night? She blushed at the mere thought of it. And was still blushing she imagined, when Daisy returned to the room with a cup and saucer.

- Mrs Coix is in the pantry, Daisy informed, standing by the armchair, hoping she'd heard her mistress rightly, but feeling doubt.

- You can sit down, Daisy, Lily said, after a few seconds waiting to see if the maid would do so automatically, but she didn't, only stood there awkwardly, like a child. Daisy sat down, arranged the cups into saucers, and began to pour the tea. She still felt awkward sitting there in front of her mistress and her mind sensed her mistress's eyes on her as she poured the tea.

-Relax, Daisy, You're a bag of nerves, Lily said, as he watched the maid's hand shake with the teapot.

- Sorry, Miss, not use to drinking tea with people like yourself, Daisy said, shyly. Having poured tea into both cups without spilling any, she looked at her mistress's hands: white, delicate, almost fragile. Lily helped herself to milk and sugar, and indicated with a gesture of her right hand for Daisy to do likewise.

- Major Wynsor and I were very close, Lily stated bluntly. I shall miss him not coming here, she added.

- I expect you will, Miss, Daisy replied in a low voice.

- His wife and I are old friends, so I expect I'll be invited to the funeral service. Though his body won't be brought back, Lily said, the latter words almost in a whisper. She sipped her tea and looked at the maid.

- What arc they going to do about the body, then, Miss? Daisy asked puzzled.

- They will bury the body out in Libya, I expect, Lily informed matter-of-factly, but inwardly wishing it wasn't so. Too far to return the body at such a time, she added, turning to gaze around the room as if Edward was there listening. She mused as her eyes wandered the room, about Edward's body. Now she would never see it again, never hold it again, against her, feel the warmth of it.

- Never seen a dead person before, Daisy uttered vaguely.

- I saw one many years ago, Lily said, breaking away from her thoughts of Edward's body.

- Did you, Miss? Daisy said, childlike in her fascination.

- Yes, Lily said, turning to gaze at her maid, a young woman, a servant of my father's, hanged herself in the woods. Lily paused. She remembered the body of the girl swaying in the slight wind, her head to one side. How old was I then? she asked herself, momentarily forgetting about Daisy sitting opposite. Seven or eight, I was, she informed herself, sitting back in the armchair, holding the cup a few inches away from her lips.

- How horrible, Daisy muttered, frowning at the thought. Why'd she do that? she asked after a few seconds reflecting on the image her mind had conjured up.

- Grief, Lily whispered as if she didn't want the maid to hear. Her boyfriend, whom she intended to marry, was killed in the Great War. She couldn't come to terms with the loss, and so she hanged herself. Lily paused again. Nanny and I discovered the body while out walking in the woods. Nanny screamed, but I just stared and tried to make sense of it.

- You don't think Major Wynsor's wife will do such a thing, do you, Miss? Daisy asked, bring her cup to her lips.

- No, of course not, Daisy, Lily said firmly. Mrs Wynsor is a Lady. Ladies don't do that kind of thing. She sipped her tea and drained the cup. Putting the cup in the saucer, she placed both down on the table. She watched as the maid did likewise, then for a few moments gazed at the girl's face.

-Have you got a gentleman friend, Daisy? Lily asked. The maid blushed and looked down at her hands.

- No, Miss, Daisy replied, but I hope to have one day. She said nothing else, but played with her fingers that were laid in her lap. Her mind closed on the thought that was about to enter her consciousness. She held it back, but an image still formed in her mind. The Major and his hands. Things he said. His whispered words. She blushed and was conscious of blushing.

-Can I go now, Miss? she asked, pushing the image of the Major from her mind as she often had to push him away from her body.

- Yes, Daisy, before Mrs Coix misses you, Lily said coolly. She had wanted to open the maid up and gather some idea what was in the girl's mind, if anything, but it wasn't going to happen she realized, and sighed inwardly, disappointed at her failure. The maid got up from the armchair and picked up the tray. Something made the maid pause. She opened her mouth to say something, but closed it again. -What is it, Daisy? Lily asked catching the opening and closing lips.

- Nothing, Miss. Only...the maid paused, her face reddened.

- What is it, Daisy? Lily asked firmly, slightly annoyed at the girl's childishness.

- The Major. He sometimes...Again, the maid paused. Lily got up from the armchair and walked to the window. The whiteness was still there, but primulas and snowdrops held their heads bravely against it all. She could hear the maid's voice, but didn't want to know what she was saying. Out in the garden she was certain she could see Edward waiting by the summerhouse, but when she looked again he was gone.

- You can go now, Daisy, Lily stated. Mrs Coix will be looking for you. She could hear the maid sigh and the rattle of the cups and saucers as the tray was moved from the room. The door closed with a dull thud. Lily brought her hands together and held them to her lips as if she were about to pray. The words of the maid drifted in and around her mind. Silly girl, she told herself, mindless fool. As if Edward would even look at the girl, she informed her mind, staring across at the grove of elms. For a moment she thought she saw a body swaying from one of the elms. The head tilted to one side, the tongue protruding rudely. Then it was gone and only a branch swayed back and forth gently as if in some dance with the breeze. Closing her eyes, she imagined Edward was behind her holding her in his arms. She wanted to sense him there, close and his warmth against her. She needed to hear his words again, his warm breath on her neck. But all she heard now were the maid's words, echoing in the still room.

Peggy Sue.

- Gilbert, the man says. Gerald Gilbert. The woman nods in acknowledgement taking in the man's cap and greyish moustache as she turns towards him. The man looks at her momentarily then returns his gaze and interest to the sea and his fishing. He would have looked at me more than once years ago, the woman thinks, watching the man lift his fishing rod higher as if it were some phallic symbol. But now she knows her looks have gone. The drink and kids did that, she muses grimly.

- Peggy Sue Sullivan, the woman says in late

reply, looking out at the sea from the end of the pier. Gerald nods his head, but says nothing for a few minutes. His mind is on the fish below, not on the woman beside him leaning on the rail a metre away. I used to bring my children here, Peggy Sue relates. Some years back now. She pictures them as they were standing about her clinging on to her skirt or holding her hand. Five of them. All grown now. Not that she sees them much now, what with the drink and all. Do you catch many fish? she asks, turning to look at the man and seeing him intent on his rod, looks away again.

- Depends, Gerald replies. Sometimes I'm lucky, other times I catch bugger all, if you'll excuse my French. He winds the reel. Of course, it's the chase that's the fun, he adds reeling again.

Peggy Sue nods and smiles. -Isn't it always, Peggy Sue says. She brushes her right hand through her greying-blonde hair and stands back from the rail. Her mouth feels dry and she thinks about looking for a pub, but decides against. She looks sideways at the man and takes in his cap and greying moustache again. She'd not give him the time of day once, but now, he held a small glimmer of hope for her. If only he'd take some interest, she muses darkly, leaning once again on the rail and staring at the sea that seems to change from blue to green and back again. Gerald reels again and then stops.

- Got away, the bugger, Gerald says moodily, reeling in quickly. He fits bait on his hook again and casts the line out into the sea. Peggy Sue watches silently looking at Gerald's hands and fingers working. Want to have a go? Gerald asks, turning to Peggy Sue and eyeing her up and down and offering her his rod.

- Never done fishing, Peggy Sue replies.

- Nothing to it, Gerald says. All in the wrist

and arms. Here, have ago, he adds. Peggy Sue shakes her head and her hair follows as her head moves from side to side.

- I'd rather watch, Peggy Sue says shyly. Gerald smiles and raises his rod skywards. The way he lifts and holds his rod makes Peggy Sue smile to herself. So much intensity, she muses. So much strength. Gerald reels gently. He lifts again.

- Do you live on the Island? Gerald asks screwing up his eyes and searching the sea for signs of fish. Peggy Sue shakes her head. She watches as the man raises the rod again.

- No, Peggy Sue replies. I just love coming here. Sort of sanctuary for me. Me and the children would come here in the summer for a day or so. She breaks off. The picture of the five children becomes painful and she looks hard at the sea. Gerald reels in fast and raises his rod high.

- Got the bugger this time, Gerald exclaims excitedly, reeling in slower now. The end of the line swings back and forth with a medium-sized fish hanging. Not too big. But still it's a catch, he says quietly to himself as much as to Peggy Sue. He unhooks the fish and throws it back again. Peggy Sue watches him and sighs.

- Why'd you throw it back? Peggy Sue asks.

- Not worth the trouble cooking, Gerald says. Plenty of fish in the sea as the saying goes. He chuckles and looks at Peggy Sue with interest for the first time. He notices her straggly greying-blonde hair and pale-blue eyes. Must have been a good-looker once, he muses to himself, gazing at her figure now held within a pink blouse and black skirt reaching just below the knees. Peggy Sue turns away her head and stares out at the sea. She feels self conscious. Feels as if the man were undressing her. She leans forward over the rail and watches as the waves hit against the pier below.

- I need a drink, Peggy Sue says. Want to come? The man says nothing at first, but puts bait on the hook slowly, intently.

- Not just yet, Gerald replies. He casts out to sea again silently. Was that a pick up? he asks himself staring out at the sea. Some years since he'd been propositioned. He'd not been bothered much since his wife had gone off. But was it worth the risk? he asks inwardly sensing the woman beside him, was it worth the bother?

- Didn't mean anything, if you're worried about it, Peggy Sue says. Just thought you'd like a drink and chat. The man nods seriously.

- All right, maybe later, Gerald says. He reels gently. He raises the rod with care. Peggy Sue studies his hands sideways. The fingers very nimble, she thinks. brushing her own fingers through her hair. Here for the day? Gerald asks, not taking his eyes from the sea.

- The weekend, Peggy Sue replies. I go back on Monday morning. Start work Tuesday. Gerald nods, but still gazes out at the sea.

- Where're you staying then? Gerald asks, reeling gently again.

- Sandown, Peggy Sue informs softly. Some guesthouse off the main road. The man nods again and turns briefly to look at her.

- How old are your children now? Gerald asks as he raises the rod skywards again. Peggy Sue folds her arms across her breast and looks along the pier as if her children were just a few metres away.

- My youngest, Ronnie, is about sixteen now and my eldest, Kate is coming up to twenty-one. I've not seen them for a few months or so, she lies and feels a stab of pain in her breast.

- Soon grow up don't they, Gerald says. He reels in slowly and raises his rod up again. Peggy Sue looks at his hands and fingers and wishes strangely she could just hold them for a few moments.

- Have you got children, then? Peggy Sue asks, still studying the man's hands and fingers. Gerald reels fast and raises his rod skywards.

- Got a bite, Gerald exclaims. His attention is focused. His mind lets the question go for a few minutes. He feels the woman close to him now. Her elbow touches his. He reels in faster still and holds the rod firmly. The line comes out of the sea and on the end a large fish sways back and forth. Now there's a big one, he says excitedly. As he reels the last few centimetres his arm brushes against the woman's arm. A warming sensation rushes through him and he feels a sudden movement within him. He unhooks the fish and stares at it in his hands. The woman looks intently at it beside him. Shall I keep it? he asks.

The woman shrugs her shoulders. - It's up to you. You caught it, Peggy Sue replies. She places her left hand on Gerald's arm gently. The man stands undecided. He looks at the fish for a few more seconds, then suddenly he throws it back over the pier into the sea. He looks down into the waves below and smiles.

- Let it live for another day, Gerald says quietly. He begins to pack his things away. Silence hangs between them. He packs. She watches for a few minutes then looks back out to sea. He finishes his packing and lifts his things onto his shoulder. Peggy Sue stands looking at him shyly. What about that drink, now? he asks. Peggy Sue pushes her fingers through her hair and stands erect.

- If you like, Peggy Sue replies. I didn't mean to sound as if I was trying to pick you up or anything. I hate drinking alone. Men always seem to get the wrong impression.

- Some men might, Gerald states as they walk along the pier together side by side, a few centimetres or so apart. I didn't answer your question just now. I've a son. About fourteen. Not seen him since he was five when the wife went off with another man. Gerald pauses. He feels a hollowness open up inside and wishes it would close again.

- Sorry, Peggy Sue says. Didn’t mean to be nosey. Didn't you get access? The man looks straight ahead as if searching the horizon for an answer.

- She went abroad. Never saw hide or hair of either of them. Gerald sounds momentarily bitter and a silence falls between them as they walk towards the Esplanade. The Esplanade is busy and crowds brush past and against them. They cross the road together, he gently guiding her arm. When they reach the other side he stands looking along the street. I know a decent bar up this side street, Gerald says, breaking the silence. Peggy Sue nods agreement and they walk slowly up the street.

Gerald brings the drinks to the table where Peggy Sue is sitting. He sits down and watches as she lifts the glass to her lips. In twenty minutes this was her third drink. He had a job to keep up with her. She'd bought the last round and he felt obliged to buy her another. She can bloody well drink all right, he muses as he looks at her opposite him. On closer study he realises she's a drinker. It's in the eyes and skin, he tells himself, lifting his glass and gazing at her. She returns his look and seems to search his face and eyes. There's a sadness there, he informs himself. Deep down.

- Get's lonely on your own, Peggy Sue says suddenly as if it had just occurred to her. Sometimes it's worse than others. Gerald looks down at his drink and searches it for an answer.

- One gets use to it. The loneliness I mean, Gerald says after a few minutes studying his glass.

- Night time's the worse, Peggy Sue says absent-mindedly looking around the bar, which is crowded. Gerald swallows hard. He feels a shiver run down his spine and his eyes lift to her face opposite.

- Can be, Gerald replies stiffly. At least sleep can put one out of one's misery. He raises his glass to his lips to stop them speaking again for a few moments. Peggy Sue looks across at Gerald and smiles.

- I suppose so, Peggy Sue says. If one were lucky to be able to sleep...If one were, she adds empathizing the word, one. Gerald puts down his glass. He watches her eyes and features.

- Are you making fun of me? Gerald says slightly uncertain of himself. He watches as she looks straight at him and smiles.

- Sorry, Peggy Sue says. Her voice is not mocking. She smiles and puts out her hand across the table towards him. Didn't mean to tease. When people speak like that it makes me feel uneasy.

Gerald nods. - Sounds off-putting, I suppose. He drinks from his glass again but looks at her intently. He isn't sure what to say next. She touches his arm with her hand now, he senses lowering the glass and studying her closely. He puts his glass on the table gently. Her hand is lying on his arm as if to detain him should he get up to leave. She's after me, he says inwardly. A feeling warms him. He realises that he suddenly wants her. He places his hand over hers and pats it a few times. Want another drink? he asks.

- Better not, Peggy Sue replies. She looks at his hand on hers. The hands are small but strong. The fingers nimble, she thinks, draining the last of her drink. Got to get back to my guesthouse for my meal. Pretty strict on mealtimes, Peggy Sue informs. Maybe another time. What about tomorrow?

- What about tonight? Gerald says.

- What about tonight? Peggy Sue says putting her glass on the table.

- A drink, Gerald says quickly. In Sandown some where? Peggy Sue looks around the bar. She shakes her head.

- Long way for you to come just for a drink, Peggy Sue says softly. She stands up and feels the room move slightly. It's up to you. She pauses. He is watching my every move, she tells herself. Watching me, watching me, she says inwardly. Up to you, she repeats as she leaves the table. Gerald watches her leave. Watches her figure as she moves away.

- Some other time maybe, Gerald says, but

she doesn't hear. She's gone. He watches the space now vacant like a car park after dark.

Daphne & Cloe.

Daphne Dryas gazed from the veranda. The May morning was bright and warm and she sensed the sun's rays on her face as she gazed out over the garden. Her husband Richard was abroad on government business and her two sons, Charles and James, were away at boarding school in Hampshire. Apart from the servants, she was alone. But not for much longer, she hoped. Soon Cloe Calluna would be arriving for what, Daphne prayed, would be a long stay.

Moving along the veranda she peered at the

mulberry tree which she loved and where, when she first met Richard, they sat and talked for hours. Now they talked little and seldom sat together for any great length of time. So it was pleasing to her that morning to know that Cloe would soon be coming and her low spirits would once again be lifted as they usually were when Cloe arrived.

Just to her right, Marsden, their head-gardener, was by the rhododendron, his balding head rising and falling in motion to his task. Down by the roses, Williams, one of the under-gardeners, was staring up at the sky. She herself would normally be down in the garden at some task or other, but today she wanted to be ready for Cloe's arrival. Just then, as she was watching Williams, a sound behind her made her turn her head. It was Nellie her personal maid.

- Mrs Calluna 'as arrived, Madam. Shall I show 'er out 'ere? Nellie said. Daphne, who despaired at times over Nellie's utterings, nodded her head.

- Yes, Nellie, and ask Mrs Wynter for refreshments, Daphne said. She watched the maid traipse along the veranda and smiled to herself. Nellie was in some ways loveable, but in others she was exasperating to the point where Daphne thought of dismissing her. But now Cloe had arrived. Her spirit lifted at the mere sound of her name and the possibilities that lay ahead.

Cloe stood by the French windows. The maid had announced her and left. Daphne was standing at the far end of the veranda smiling at her.

- So nice to see you again, Cloe, Daphne said. Left your husband at home, I hope.

Cloe nodded and smiled. - He's gone to Scotland for a few weeks. Some professor wants him to lecture on Locke and Hobbes or someone or other, Cloe informed moving along the veranda where Daphne stood. I couldn't wait for him to leave...And the thought of us together again.

Daphne embraced her and kissed her cheek. Then Daphne stood back and studied her friend closely. Cloe was about six inches shorter and slimmer; her hair was as dark as night. Her eyes were hazel and her face petite.
- May Scotland keep him, and I, you, Daphne whispered as she embraced Cloe again.

- Glad Richard's away, too. Have I my favourite room? Cloe said.

Daphne nodded. Taking her friend's hand she led her in through the French windows and out of sight of Williams who stood scratching his head beneath the hot May sun.

Cloe stood by the window. Daphne had left her to freshen up and now she looked out on to the vast garden below. Behind her the room, which she felt was her room, and in which, over the years, she had grown to love and feel as some kind of sanctuary from the external world and her domestic responsibilities. Just to her right she could see an avenue of pinus trees, which led off to an area of shrubbery where she and Daphne often in the past, could lose themselves and be alone together.

The click of a door sounded behind her and she turned. A young maid stood by the door her hands held before her as if in prayer.

- Mrs Dryas said to see if there was anyfink to needed, Madam, the maid said.

Cloe studied the girl for a few seconds then shook her head. - No, I have all that I need, Cloe said. The maid made an attempted curtsey and closed the door softly behind her. Eliot, her husband, suggested she bring her personal maid, Betty; but she didn't want any spies along with her when she stayed with Daphne. Servants were infamous for their gossip below stairs...She never felt at ease with Betty around; it seemed if she were constantly watching her and reporting back to Eliot. I'm becoming paranoid, she whispered turning back to the window. She longed for Daphne to be here beside her again...She wondered if Daphne's husband had spies in the household watching her, observing her every move and word as she was certain Eliot did. Down by the roses a gardener was looking up at the window, he was mopping his brow with an off-white rag as if the May sun was too much for him. Cloe turned from the window away from his eyes.

Daphne waited by the sundial. She had told Nellie to inform Cloe of her whereabouts. The red roses surrounding the sundial, which were themselves edged in by box hedging, formed a cross. She walked around the dial until she had found the time given. Cloe seemed on edge she felt. Something was bothering her, Daphne thought as she moved around the sundial again. She thought it something to do with Eliot; there was something about the man she found tiresome and irritating on the few occasions she'd met him. Husbands, she mused, are a necessary evil. If she could have had her children without Richard she would have been happy, and to have Cloe too would be heaven on earth...But things weren't done that way. Such a social scandal would ruin her and Cloe and blight her sons' lives. She sighed and walked once more round the sundial.

The pergola was alive with white roses. Daphne and Cloe walked beneath surrounded by scent and the sun's heat. - You seem anxious, Cloe dear, Daphne said. Can I help?

- I think Eliot's spying on me, Cloe informed in a whisper. Daphne looked at her friend with a frown. Then Cloe told her all that had happened since their last meeting a few months before. By the time all was told they had reached the small white summerhouse. They entered and the cool air eased them and they embraced and kissed, irrespective of possible spies on looking.

Cloe looked out at the night sky. The day had past off pleasantly, she and Daphne had been able to be alone occasionally, which was what she herself so much needed. After late dinner she had played some Bach on the piano for Daphne; then they had walked into the garden and enjoyed the warm May evening amongst the shrubs and flowers.

If only I could relax about being spied on, she mused, looking up at the stars and bright moon. She was sure the servants were talking about them and about her especially. Everywhere she went one of them was looking or whispering, she was certain. Eliot had his ways and the means to have her watched, as if she was untrustworthy and he suspected her of having an affair…

There was a slight knock at the door. The door opened and Daphne entered. - Are you all right? Daphne whispered, closing the door behind her.

- Yes, Cloe replied. Just watching the evening sky. Daphne nodded and went to stand beside her at the window. Her body ached to hold Cloe, but she held back.

- Is there anything you need? Daphne enquired.

- Only you, Cloe whispered, feeling Daphne's arm near her own.

- I’m here, my dear, Daphne informed warmly. Cloe seemed troubled.

- It’s too risky, Cloe uttered quietly, as if afraid others were listening. The servants may talk, she added, looking past Daphnc at the closed door.

- The servants are not about; I've dismissed them, Daphne said. Anyway, I know my servants; they will say nothing even if they did suspect something...Least of all to Richard. Daphne smiled. Cloe didn't seem convinced and shook her head.

- One never knows with servants, Cloe muttered. Who pays the piper selects the melody. It's Richard who pays them not you...Eliot too knows the power of money and the influence fear can have. Cloe went to the bed and sat on the edge.

- Love and loyalty are stronger, Daphne suggested, softly. Nellie, for all her funny ways and language, is loyal to me alone. She would tell me if any were untrustworthy or were being disloyal. Cloe put her hands over her face. She shook her head and mumbled words, which Daphne couldn't understand. She sat down beside Cloe and placed her arm about her. Eliot has no power or influence here, Daphne stated firmly, yet gently.

- I'm sorry for being such a fool, Cloe said. She took her hands away from her face and laid them in her lap. You are right; he can have no spies here. She laid her head on Daphne's shoulder and closed her eyes. She wanted so much to be here always, like this, secure and loved, but deep within she knew it could never be, and that these snatched moments were all that they would ever have together no matter how hard she prayed. They lay back on the bed and embraced, but still Cloe listened for footsteps and whispered words, outside the room.

Sunlight suddenly entered the room. The maid had opened the shutters silently and had turned towards the bed. Cloe placed her right hand up to her eyes to ward off the brightness. - What time is it? she said with a yawn.

The maid frowned. - About nine, Madam, Nellie replied. Mrs Dryas sent me up ta open up the shutters and see if you were all right, Nellie added, standing momentarily to attention. Cloe sat upright in bed and studied the maid for a few moments. And asked if you'd like yer breakfast in bed or wevver you'd like ta come down ta the breakfast room? Nellie appended slowly, putting her hands behind her back.

- I'll come down later, Cloe said slowly, still scrutinizing the maid. The maid attempted a curtsey and moved away from the bed. Wait, Cloe said. Were you outside in the passageway last night, listening? The maid frowned and shook her head.

- No, Madam. Mrs Dryas sent us all off ta bed early last night, Nellie replied, puzzled. Cloe closed her eyes and lay back in the bed. She gestured with her hand a sign of dismissal and the maid left the room flummoxed and clueless with a slight click of the door.

Daphne sat in the breakfast room. She contemplated Cloe sitting in silence opposite her. Apart from a weak, Good morning, Cloe had said nothing for the five minutes following. Daphne ate with little interest; Cloe ate hardly anything at all, just sipped her tea and poked at the breakfast with her fork.

- Sleep well? Daphne asked, softly. Cloe raised her eyes to Daphne's face and shook her head.

- Slept little after you left, Cloe whispered. I'm sure someone was in the passageway during the night, she added even quieter.

Daphne expressed puzzlement. Pouring more tea and lifting her head, she waved away a young maid from the room. - We will be all right for a while, Ena. The maid curtsied and left the room. Looking at Cloe, she said, There was no one about, Cloe. You must get this spying nonsense out of your head.

Cloe threw down her cutlery. - Perhaps I should leave, Cloe said, rising from the table. You think I'm imagining it all; you don't understand.

Daphne rose from the table and went to Cloe's side. - Calm yourself. I don't want you to leave, but I can assure you no one here was in the passageway last night, Daphne stated. Cloe sat down and hid her face in her hands. Daphne patted her shoulder. I don't know what Eliot has done or said to put you in this state, but here you are safe, Daphne said gently.

Cloe sobbed. Daphne didn't know Eliot as well as she thought. She could be safe nowhere, she was convinced of that. The maid in her room, the gardener, others watching...But what if Daphne was right? Maybe I am becoming paranoid. Maybe Eliot has driven close to madness. She stopped sobbing and moved her hands from her face.

- Are you sure I'm safe here? Cloe uttered like a frightened child. Daphne squeezed her tight and nodded her head in affirmation.

They walked in the garden. Daphne's arm

linked with Cloe's as they wandered beneath the pergola heavy with white roses. Cloe had become brighter and Daphne was pleased that the day had provided them with many opportunities to be alone together. Lunch had gone well and after an afternoon nap they had ventured outside for a tour of the grounds.

- I shall miss you when you leave, Daphne said suddenly as they paused at the far end of the pergola. Cloe bit her lip. She squeezed Daphne's arm and held back tears that were waiting to fall.

- I shall miss you, too, Cloe whispered. She felt a sudden sinking feeling inside her and had a sensation as if she were drowning.

- Must you leave so soon? Daphne asked.

- Eliot's letter this morning was unambiguous about my returning, Cloe informed. She had screwed up the letter and cursed him, but she knew she had to return home. Here was her happiness, but it was to be left behind. She had no choice. Eliot was sending their chauffeur the next morning to take her back. She squeezed Daphne's arm tighter, but the sinking feeling remained, pulling her down and down and down.

Daphne waved as the car drove away. Cloe's face became smaller and smaller until it disappeared from sight. She had been silent until the last hour, then she had sobbed. The time has gone so quickly, Daphne mused sadly. Poor Cloe. And she remembered their last night together and the hesitant lovemaking, the listening for sounds; the whispered fears. Now she had left, when they would meet again, Daphne didn’t know.

- ‘as she gone now, Madam? Nellie asked at Daphne's side.

- Yes, Nellie, she's gone, Daphne replied. She gazed up the drive in a vain hope that maybe Cloe might return, but she knew she wouldn't.

Deep down inside she felt she might never see Cloe again, as if somehow it was fated that way. She turned away from the drive and walked with Nellie along the path and into the garden.

Daphne sat up in bed. She gazed at the maid by the window. -What are you doing there, Nellie? she asked quietly.

- Looking at the stars and that silvery moon, Nellie replied. She stood naked with her hands resting on her hips. Her dark-black hair let loose on her back.

- Come back to bed, Daphne pleaded, I'm getting cold. She pulled back the covers and waited until the maid tiptoed back and into bed again.

- Bet you miss 'er, don't yer Madam, Nellie whispered.

- Yes, Daphne replied with a sigh. She drew Nellie towards her and kissed her cheek. But you are here always, Nellie, Daphne said softly. Nellie smiled. She was safe again. Where she belonged. Daphne listened, but there were no footsteps or whispering voice tonight. Poor Cloe. Poor poor Cloe.

Concepta's Remembrance.

We are commanded by the fourth Commandment to love obey and reverence the parents in all that is not sin Concepta Connell remembers Father Burke saying when she was a young girl and had the father come to the house and tell her the way of things when her mother had gone to the father and said she'd been disobedient and had not been doing as she was told despite her da giving her backside the size of his hand and the lash of his tongue and sending her to the bedroom without the supper and the lights out and now sitting in Donovan's bar beside

Davy Doyle the sudden remembrance of the old priest with his hat in his hand and his dark eyes peering into her eyes and soul brings a smile to her lips yet not of mockery or disrespect but how things were then with the Church and the priests and her parents thinking that the father bless his old hat and eyes could have solved anything at all with regards to her and her finding her way in the new world breaking out inside of her and with the burning of bras and throwing away of morals not that she considered herself a bad girl as such or one of those loose women her mother had always gone on about over dinner with her da looking at her mother as if she'd lost her mind and wanting her to close her mouth with the words and stuff the food in the hole and chew herself to silence but she seldom did Concepta remembers always the one with the words and judgements and the pointing finger even in the shops when she was supposed to be shopping and gathering the goods for the home and Da bless his rural ways and porter soaked skin would walk behind her with the heavy sighs and raised eyes to Heaven and wanting the time to shift to get himself to the bar and lift his porter to lips before the angels came or dark Death with his scythe to cut him down like the wheat in the fields and as Davy offers her the cigarette and lights it with his own and gives her the wink promising a good time ahead if she could get him home sober enough she looks beyond him at the seat where her da once sat in the corner with his pint of porter and his pals and the laugh deep and heavy as peat and the pipe stuck in his mouth and the cap on his head pushed back revealing the receding hairline and the scar on the forehead where a stone thrown by some idjit Protestant had struck him as boy and she looks away and feels Davy put his hand on her thigh and push back and forth his fingers warm and kindly and she looks him in the eyes the bright blue eyes the eyes of an angel her mother had said once when the gin had softened her tongue and heart before the demons of dementia came and stole her mind and left her childlike in her ways and means and words and Davy pushes his hand further up her thigh and she senses her flesh tingle the skin suddenly coming to life as if it had been asleep for a thousand years and his look and his smile and the cigarette hanging there at the corner of his mouth like some suicidal fool ready for the jump and the nose of him like a noble thing stuck there on a face of a peasant on the features of some loon yet she loves him with all her heart and flesh and wants the clock to ticktockticktock her and him home to the bed and the lights out and the church bells to chime the time and the features of Father Burke altering into the sweet Davy Doyle with his masterly ways and the lovemaking talent to bring her to her knees and the rockabye baby passion that will always please.

Easy to Remember.

- Women like you make me sick, the young blonde says as she moves quickly away. She disappears into the crowds and I've lost her. There's not much one can do when another's beauty captures one's mind and soaks up each moment with the thinking of them and wanting of them. But in the end all you can do is hope that this particular one will be the right one and won't scamper off like some frightened mouse. In this case, I'd got it wrong. Nonetheless, she was beautiful and is gone. I, too, was beautiful once, as Judy would admit if she were here and not buried up in some London graveyard with moss and weeds over her small stone. I'll make her a visit tomorrow and talk like the old times, if the weather holds.

* * *

We walked along the beach in our cotton dresses and bare feet. The cold waves rushed over our feet and made us scream with delight. We held hands and ran further along. Then we stood and looked out at the horizon to where the sea seemed to disappear. The beach was deserted, save for an old man and his dog in the far distance.

- Can’t believe I'm fourteen tomorrow, Judy said. I’ll be the same age as you then, she added. I could feel the warmth of her hand in mine and squeezed it gently. She turned to face me. Her hazel eyes searched mine and after a minute or so she leaned forward and kissed me on the lips. If my mum or dad could see us now, Pru, I'd be dead, she said smiling. I took her hand and we moved further into the sea until the water was near our knees and our dresses were getting damp. We ran back to the sand with our free hands holding up our dampened dresses. Then we stood looking up the beach at the approaching man and his dog wondering what he thought and not giving a damned fig what he thought.

The old man passed in silence. His dog sniffed us, then moved on as if we weren't worth another sniff. When he was well passed us, I turned to Judy and said,- I love sunsets. The sun was sitting on the horizon like a huge orange and a few clouds moved by it cutting it in two. Judy said she loved them too and we stood and watched until the chill bit into us and we moved back along the beach, towards the boarding house where our parents were waiting anxiously no doubt, as the dark gradually crept in after us.

* * *

The cemetery is silent and almost deserted. I wander along paths until I come to where I think her stone is. Its smallness is how I know it. Her name is still visible as I rub away the moss and pull the weeds. JUDY TYSON. PASSED PEACEFULLY. !948-1984. I sit on the warm grass and stare at the stone. - I'm here, Judy, I say. I came on impulse. It takes time to understand her silence. Been rejected again. Blonde this time. Beauty, she was. I look around the cemetery. A few people pass some distance away. The sun is warm above me. Clouds scarce and white. You'd love this weather. I break off and look down at the grass. Tomorrow I'm going back to that beach. You remember that beach? I sense her. She remembers. She remembers.

* * *

Mr and Mrs Tyson and my parents were walking the gardens just off the beach past the pier. Judy and I remained behind with promises not to wander far. - That's them out of the way, Judy said with a sigh. She looked at me with those hazel eyes and smiled. Where shall we go?

- Along by the cliff; there we could be alone, I said. She agreed and we walked along the beach, past the crowds with their children and deckchairs and balls, along the narrow spaces between large rocks until we found the path that led up to the cliffs. There was no one about; we were alone. We walked up slowly until we reach half way up the cliff. There we stood looking out to sea. We stared in silence; each of us occupied by our own thoughts. I felt her hand touch mine; wrapped itself around mine softly. Beautiful, isn't it, I said, the sea. Judy said it was and that she wanted to go where the sea ended and take me with her. Far from our parents, she stated, far from interference and judgements. Below waves rushed to the shore and above us seagulls moved and made noise that didn't manage to break the spell of the moment. I sensed the closeness of her body and saw out of the corner of my eye her brown hair touched slightly by a mild breeze.

- Shall we walk the shoreline this evening again? Judy asked.

- Yes. Let's see the sunset, I said. I felt her

kiss my cheek and a warm glow flowed through me, and I knew I never wanted to be parted from her. We walked up further, getting slower the steeper it became, until we reach the top. We stared out at the sea again. Now we heard voices behind us and knew we were not alone anymore. Our hands parted. We said nothing; just gazcd in our own silence.

* * *

The boarding house still stands thirty years after our last visit. It looks smaller and less proud. My heart pounds within me as if I'd seen a ghost walk. I pass by and do not enter. The road is wider now that separates the boarding house from the beach. Cars file past slowly. Crowds of holidaymakers stream past each with their own lives and desires. I cross the road and stand on the edge of the beach; the sands are dirtier and crowded. The noise is disturbing, the smell uninviting. I move between the bodies and walk further along the sands towards the cliffs. The path up the cliff is still there, but slightly overgrown. Few people have ventured along this part and I sense a calm enter me. I sit on a large rock near by and look out to sea. - I'm back, Judy, I say. My voice sounds hollow, empty. Wish you were here, I add, feeling foolish. I sense nothing of her. The waves rush in noisily. Maybe it was a mistake to come back here, I say internally lowering my head and closing my eyes. I hear the seagulls, but feel no hand in mine, or her presence.

* * *

From Judy's room in the boarding house we could see far out to where the sea met the wide horizon. Our parents were out, leaving us reluctantly behind, as they toured a local historical spot. We were by the window together, Judy peering out of her father's black binoculars towards the horizon.

- How long before they're back? I asked.

She shrugged her shoulders - Don't know; quite a time, I hope, she said lowering the binoculars. She offered them to me, but I declined. She put them on the old chair beside the window, and taking my hand led me to her small single bed with its pink bed cover. We sat down and for a few moments said nothing. Then she bounced on the bed and said, - Will you get in bed with me? I frowned and stared at her like a loon.

- What do you mean? I asked. She patted the bed with her right hand.

- I want to hold you and kiss you, she said quietly. I looked at the bed and then at her. I felt unsure of what she wanted of me.

- Can't we do that sitting here? I asked. I felt my body tingle. A slow wave of feeling moved through me.

- Yes, she replied, but I want to hold you naked, flesh-to-flesh. I want to lie beside you and hear your heart beat. She gazed at me and I breathed in deeply sensing her closeness.

- All right, I said. I was nervous and shy. But what if our parents come back and find us? I asked. She laughed and said they'd be ages and besides we could always put the chair under the doorknob to keep them out. The thought of it made me laugh and I relaxed. We undressed slowly putting our clothes on the floor and climbed into the small bed together. There was little space, so we lay close together, our bodies warm against each other. We kissed. The far off sea was soundless. The seagulls were absent from above our heads and only the soft creek of the bed as we moved, betrayed our presence to the far away outside world.

* * *

I wander alone along the beach, holding my shoes, walking barefoot so that the surf can wash over them as the tide rolls in. The crowds have returned to their homes or guest houses or hotels and, except for the occasional couple, the beach is deserted. I stop and look out to sea. The sunset reminds me of those two weeks in 1962. Only there is no Judy beside me holding my hand. No words to share; no memories to laugh over. The day has been depressing: I have not felt Judy's presence as I had hoped. Even now standing on the beach, I do not sense her presence. The feel the slight wind. I hear only the sea.

- Lovely sunset. I turn to see where the soft voice has come from and there stands a woman in a flowered cotton dress and bare feet.

- Yes, I say. The woman moves beside me and gazes out at the dark green sea.

- I come every year, she says, still gazing out at the horizon.

- Lucky you, I reply. I haven't been here since I was a fourteen-year old girl. She turns and smiles. Her eyes are hazel and her look warms me.

- That’s a long time to wait to return, she says, softly.

- I came to find something, I say quietly. She nods and turns to face the sea again.

- Did you find what you were looking for? she asks.

- No. I shouldn't have come back, it was a mistake. I look down at the damp sand and push my toes into it. Easy to remember, I whisper, washing my toes in the incoming water.

- Hard to forget, the woman says. We look at each other in silence. We move along, letting the waves wash over our feet and she begins to laugh. I haven't done this since I was young, she says as if she were a child again.

- Neither have I, I say shyly. She tells me she's staying at the boarding house and comes every year. I tell her I have a room at the Pier Hotel and was only staying for a few days. When I ask her about the boarding house, she says she has a room looking down on to the beach. That was Judy's room I tell myself as we stop and look at the sunset once more.

- Will you have dinner with me tonight? The woman asks suddenly. I know it's presumptuous, but please say, yes.

I feel uneasy at first and feel I should decline. Her hazel eyes are searching me in a way that reminds me of Judy.- Yes, all right. Where? I ask. She suggests a restaurant she knows and says where and when to meet her. Then smiling she turns and walks along the beach, her cotton dress moving gently like a sail in a calm wind, until she disappears from sight.

* * *

- It’s our last sunset, Judy said. We had stop by the rocks and were peering out at the sun, which sat like a huge orange balloon on the far away sea. I wish it would never end. I hate going back to London after this, she said moodily. She sighed. Her hand squeezed mine. Her flesh against mine. Our naked feet on the sands, wet from our soaking walk.

- I want to come here again with you, I uttered emotionally. She turned and nodded. Her eyes had tears in them that made the hazel colour look darker. Hold me, I said. She did. Held me tightly.

- Remember this sunset. Remember us here. This is our eternity. Her words echoed against my cheek and I felt the dampness of her tears. We kissed. Her lips on mine. Mine on hers, wet, soft.

- Easy to remember, I said. We moved away from each other and stood back. Hard to forget. She looked around to see if we were alone. We were. The beach was totally deserted and the sky was slowly darkening. We wandered back along the beach hand in hand in silence. No more words. No more sunsets. Only the lonely walk back to the boarding house for the last time.

*****

I sit opposite the woman in the restaurant she had suggested. She had been waiting for me outside and when I arrived she seemed so pleased as if I were an old friend she hadn't seen for years. Her hazel eyes search me as we eat, and I feel so relieved that all is so natural and not strained as meetings between strangers usually are. Putting down her cutlery for a few moments, she asks if I would walk with her along the beach before the evening ended. I say I will, and I am glad of the opportunity to see the evening sky again.

- Look at that moon, the woman says as we

walk on the beach. The air is calm and warm. We stand and look up at the sky and the bright glowing moon. Those stars, they make the universe seem so immense and us so small. Her words echo round us. I want to reach out, take hold of the words, and keep them. Her voice seems familiar, yet I cannot place it.

- One cannot see where the sea ends in the dark, I say. We lower our eyes and stare out to where the sound of the sea rushes towards us. I become aware that her left hand has taken hold of mine and she is squeezing it gently. I let the touch invade me. I sense her flesh on mine and am pleased. T.S. Eliot wrote that the sea has many voices, I say wanting her hand not to release mine.

- And Conrad said that the works of the sea are a mystery. I love the sea. Love the sound and smell of it. Love the feel of it on my flesh, the woman says, her voice close to my cheek as she leans her head next to mine.

- You haven't told me your name, I say suddenly, fearing her departure and not knowing what to call her if...She releases my hand and turns towards me. She whispers in my ear, her words soft like snow. I stare at her and sense my heart pound within me. We say nothing more and start to walk along the beach again. It seems as if we are alone in the universe, just us two. Even the sea has become silent and rushes forward as if in mime to embrace us, to swallow us up into its cold arms.

We enter her room in the boarding house silently. She switches on the light to dispel the darkness and the room seems as it was thirty years ago. Yet some things have changed. The wallpaper is brighter. The pictures are different on the walls. The bed is new with an orange duvet. - I was here thirty years ago, I whisper.

- So was I, the woman says. She walks to the

bed and sits down. I feel so strange. I stand staring around the room and then lower my eyes and look at her sitting there so calm, so unperturbed. Come on, Pru, sit here with me, she says softly, tapping the space on the bed beside her. I walk towards her and sit where she suggests.

- Deja vu, I whisper. Is this real? I ask. She lays her head on my shoulder and her voice seems to enter my body.

- Hesse says, there is no reality except the one within us. This reality, Pru. This is our eternity, her voice says. We are in darkness. We undress. We are side by side, flesh to flesh, as if nothing had changed, as if today was always today, ad infinitum.

The Sacred Lake.

He is sitting by the murky pond with a fishing rod held between his legs like some phallic symbol and the line is immersed in the dark-brown water, looking lifeless. He doesn't notice me standing by the trees some metres back. His body, slim, arched, is alive only to the dark dank pond before him. Making my way down from the trees on to the grass about the pond I am hoping he will turn and take note of me, but he doesn't. It isn't until I am a metre away that he finally turns his head and gives me a quick glance. His eyes, greyish-blue, search me up and down, until eventually they settle on my knees that show beneath my short skirt.

Sit down if you're staying; I can't bear people standing around me when I'm fishing, he says in a deep voice. I sit down with effort on the grass, my left hand giving me balance. He gives me another quick glance then turns his head once more to the dark water before us. I'm Sorbus Ash, he says, my father owns the Ash Stables. He indicates with a toss of his head and I look to where his head seems to indicate.

I’m Abelia Hardwood, I reply, pulling my skirt down as far as possible over my knees.

You live in Weststead cottage don't you? he asks.

Yes, I reply, we've been there about a three month now. He moves the rod between his hands and settles it again.

I’ve seen you about with Betula Birch, he states, his eyes firmly focusing on the pond. I watch him for a few minutes; looking at his hands; at his face, pale, and his hair blonde-white brushed back without care or style. He turns and stares at me. Betula’s mother is a strange woman, he informs. She is not one to cross. He then becomes silent and for a few more minutes and I sit watching him, his rod and the water alternatively, beginning to feel awkward.

Do you catch many fish here? I ask to break the awkward silence.

Seldom, he replies. Then after five minutes silence he begins to tell me all about Betula and her mother and matters of the past. I listen in silence, watching his lips move, his eyes occasionally settling on me, and wonder what he's thinking. Then he stops and resumes his silence. He raises the rod between his legs again and then settles the line back into the water. I sit up and rest down on my heels giving him a quick glance to see if he is watching me, but he isn't. He seems too focused on the pond to even be aware any longer that I am here. I stand up and prepare to leave.

I must be going, I say, looking at his head now beneath me.

He nods. Careful how you go; it gets quite slippery up there, he says in return, looking at me as I turn to go.

Hope you get lucky, I say, nodding towards the pond.

I seldom do, he says, looking at me as I walk up the bank. When I look back he is looking once more at the murky waters of the pond and I have now left his consciousness like a passing thought.

Betula Birch sits by the pond with her arms around her legs, her chin resting on her knees. She seems in deep thought. I sit about half a metre away from her looking at her light-brown hair, long and straight, and her face pale-white, her eyes hazel. Something about her captivated me some months back and still does; captivates me in a way I have never been captivated before. She smiles. Her lips fill out as she smiles and turns her head towards me.

You know what I have decided to call this place, Abelia? she says, her voice full of mystery.

No, I reply, moving a little closer to her. What? She takes her right hand from her knees and puts it on my arm with the gentlest touch.

The Sacred Lake, she says excitedly. Our lake.

Sacred? I say.

Special and magic. At least to you and me, she says clutching my arm tighter. I nod and look out at the muddy pond. Doesn't seem too sacred to me, but I say nothing, only nod more. We must always come here and renew our friendship...Years to come...Promise? she looks at me, her eyes almost pleading for my reply.

Yes, I promise. Let our friendship never need renewing though, I add putting my hand over hers on my arm. She smiles and leans forward and kisses my cheek.

Abelia, I hope so too, she says like a converted lost soul. We sit in silence side by side for what seems ages, then she says, Don’t ever come here with anyone else. Promise me that?

I can't promise, I inform quietly. She looks at me momentarily as if I had slapped her.

Why can't you? she asks, her voice pained.

I came here yesterday and met a young man, I say hesitantly. She removes her hand from my arm and folds it against her breast with her other hand like two frightened birds.

What man? she asks me, her voice rising, her eyes darkening.

Said his name was Sorbus Ash, I inform, feeling apprehensive.

Sorbus was here? she says. She stares at me, then looks away at the pond. Bet he was fishing, she says without turning her head.

Yes, but I didn't know he'd be here, I inform seeking to excuse myself, although not knowing why. She sighs and moves away from me a few centimetres as some kind of gesture. I feel as if someone is turning their hand inside of me wrenching at my intestines. I sense tears in my eyes and a huge lump like an orange in my throat. After a few minutes of complete silence, she turns and looks at me.

You can't trust men, she says. Always the same lies, always the same wants. She shakes her head and sighs again. Thought you were different, she says, but you're just the same as all those others enthralled by men and their lies.

Don’t say that, Betula, I cry, I'm not hiding anything from you; Sorbus Ash means nothing to me. She sniffs the air and then breathes out heavily as if casting out demons.

What'd he say, then? she asks.

I tell her all I can remember about what Sorbus had told me the day before. She sighs, then looks away at the pond. Silence fills the air. I feel momentarily like one in exile or in that place called Limbo I've heard about. Then she turns to me and smiles.

I was too quick to judge you, she says. Sorry, am I forgiven?

Nothing to forgive, I say. She leans towards me and kisses my cheek again. We sit in silence gazing out at the waters of our Sacred Lake as the sunlight breaks through the branches of the trees above as if to bless us like two children unaware of our innocence.

*

As we leave the Sacred Lake it begins to rain and we run hand in hand, laughing and screaming, as our hair and clothes cling to us like damp second skins.

Come on, Abelia, she says, let's get to the woods before we drown. I nod as we rush side by side, laughing even louder, and the rain coming down faster and harder. Isn't it beautiful, she says excitedly, as we look up at the darkening sky and nearing the fence that separates the field from the woods.

You're mad, I say. You're like a drowned cat. She laughs and her eyes appear almost green like emeralds.

*

We clamber over the fence and into the woods where we run along the narrow path still laughing, but quietly now, a sense of calmness entering our minds. After a few minutes, Betula stops suddenly and taking my hands she leans forward and kisses me on the lips. We part and stare at each other; at damp hair; at faces flushed with running; into eyes that seem deep as oceans.

Wish this moment could last for ever, Betula says quietly, her lips a few centimetres away.

So do I, I say, searching her hazel eyes, seemingly green.

Seldom have I felt so alive, she says in a whisper, clutching my hands tightly in hers. I think I see tears in her eyes and want to touch them, but don't. We stand for what seems ages, but is possibly only minutes, and then walk on along the path towards my parent's cottage in a tense silence.

*

I sit by the Sacred Lake alone looking at the murky water, wondering if Betula will be able to come or not. It looks like rain as it did seven days ago when Betula and I were here last. Maybe she won't be able to come, I think, lifting my eyes to the sky between the branches of the trees over head. If her mother knew what her fourteen-year-old daughter and I got up to last Sunday she'd never let her out again, that's if she hadn't killed her, I muse, watching the branches swaying above me. My mother too, I tell myself, closing my eyes for a few seconds, to capture Betula's face, but fail.

We had arrived at the cottage like drenched kittens. My mother said we had better go up to my room and change into something dry while she prepared tea and our clothes dried in the airing cupboard. So we went upstairs to my bedroom and peeled off our second skins. And it was then, while we stood momentarily naked, that we looked at each other and a sense of strangeness came over me. Betula stood, her hands over her breasts, gazing at me with her eyes now hazel, not green. She moved her hands away from her breasts and took my right hand in hers and drew me close to her.

A movement to my side causes me to turn and

Sorbus Ash stands by the trees above the pond. He looks at me for a few moments in silence, then comes down through the undergrowth towards me slowly.

All alone? he asks, brushing his fishing rod around him like a lance.

I'm waiting for Betula, I reply, feeling disturbed. She said she'd meet me here.

Bet she doesn't, he says sitting on the ground a metre away, placing his rod beside him. Her mother seldom let's her out, except for school and church, he adds. I watch him undo his rod and prepare it for fishing, feeling uneasy, wishing Betula would come and prove him wrong. And as I watch him, I wonder what he would think if he knew what Betula and I did last Sunday, then dismiss the thought as it makes me feel... Well...best not go into that now. He casts out and the line hits the water causing a series of ripples to flow out from the place where the hook and worm enter.

Ripples, yes, ripples, I muse, sitting back, folding my arms around my legs, resting my chin on my knees, ripples would certainly flow out if anyone knew what we did last Sunday. I smile briefly to myself and stare at the centre of the ripples.

You were here with her last Sunday weren't you? Sorbus says suddenly, breaking the silence.

How do you know? I say, caught off guard and blushing mildly.

Saw you, he mutters. I look at him as he sighs. Strange pair, you two, he says. I look away and stare at the water again.

We like it here, I say. I almost tell him that it's our Sacred Lake, but hold my tongue. He'll think we're mad, I tell myself, closing my eyes, wanting to capture Betula's face, but again failing.

Like mother, like daughter, he says in a

drone. Then he says nothing, letting a silence settle about us. I remember the kiss Betula gave me last Sunday as we lay on my bed, my eyes still closed, wishing she was here now, kissing, knowing she won't come, not now.

Betula never came yesterday. And I could tell from the way Sorbus looked and acted that he was pleased for some damned reason. Now as I sit here by our Lake again, I hope she comes and sits here with me and relieves me of this pent up feeling inside. A week ago we were here and apart from the time we spend together at school, I've not seen her alone since. I recall last Sunday afternoon and feel a great need for Betula to be here now. How, while my mother prepared tea, Betula and I lay naked on my bed doing the kind of things I'd never knew you could do.

Did you think I wasn't going to come? Sorbus says, disturbing my thoughts, carrying his rod and bag.

Wasn’t waiting for you, I retort. I’m waiting for Betula.

She’ll not come; he says coolly, her mother won't let her out.

Why not? I say feeling anger rise in me. He shrugs his shoulders and unpacks his rod. He pulls it from the long bag and begins to look for bait. Why the hell won't she let her come? I ask louder, disturbing the silence about us.

Strange woman, her mother, he says, pushing a worm on to the hook.

He says nothing more, but casts out and the hook plops into the murky water of our Lake. I sense an ache in my stomach and wish Betula would come and prove Sorbus wrong. I sit forward my head against my knees and close my eyes. How can I go on like this? Where is she? The thoughts race round my head like frightened mice. In addition, all I can hear is Sorbus a few metres away murmuring to himself and birds up in the branches making their sounds; all I want to hear is Betula's voice saying something into my ear or just the sound of her breathing beside me.

But nothing of her comes and I open my eyes and see Sorbus standing, pulling and winding in his line. His face is paler than usual and he has a determined look about his features as if he had caught something far larger than he had ever anticipated. I watch him for some seconds, then turn to where his line is dragging against the dark waters. Ripples rush away from his catch as he winds in frantically, his face becoming paler and paler, his breathing strained. Then we both see it; large, dark, like some huge drowned cat moving against the water's skin.

What is it? he says anxiously, as the dark thing moves closer to us. The darkness becomes suddenly lighter and light-brown hair, matted, damp, clings across a white mask as it moves ever closer to the edge of the pond. Sorbus stops winding and drops the rod. He turns and vomits into some bushes behind him, the sounds haunting.

It’s a body, I exclaim disbelievingly, clutching my hands together in a gesture of praying. The face, pale, lifeless, drifts and then thuds noiselessly against the edge of the pond. Sorbus, arching over the bushes, is senseless to my words.   It's Betula, I whisper, Betula. But the words seem senseless to me, too. I remember last Sunday and that kiss she gave as we lay upon my bed and the look in her hazel eyes... The eyes are now closed, but there lurks about her lips, bluish like a bruise, a promise of a kiss, not delivered, but promised like one blown from a hand from some far off place at some later date, when the lips once again become moist and crimson.

*

Sorbus will never fish here again, or so he says.

Betula's body rests elsewhere now, her bloated flesh fished from the pond some weeks back. But to me sitting quietly at the edge of our Sacred Lake, she's here by my side, noiseless, restful.

It's very tempting to join her as she beckons me with her pale-white finger and whisperings. I remember that kiss some Sunday back as we lay naked on my bed...But it seems ages ago... And the water seems so cold like kissing the lips of one who has died... But the embrace, so wanted, so needed, calms and I drift, noiseless, like a leaf to where Betula whispers and beckons to me from within our Sacred Lake.

Duck Pond.

Now is the winter of our discontent made glorious summer by this sun of York. You don't know why those words should come to you, now, as you move carefully through the undergrowth towards the duck pond. It was those words that Thomas often quoted and others when you were alone together by this murky pond. And as you tread carefully now, you remember that once you and he would run down here towards the pond as if it were some kind of paradise. Here you could be alone together. Away from the eyes of parents and friends. Alone to just be together, to be what you were.

Emily, Thomas would say aloud, here we can be what we are. And he would run ahead and stand on the edge of the pond peering into the dark depths. See, those waters, he went on, turning round to see where you were, see how the reflections of the sky and trees above are so well done. As if painted by Monet or such. And he would become silent as if he were meditating upon the words he spoke.

You stand on the edge and stare upon the motionless murky water. The dark reflection of the sky and trees above are different now. The trees have overgrown and have drawn shadows with them. You squat down as if to sit, but don't. Instead, you crouch there and stare ahead as if you expect Thomas to appear at any minute and wave. But what you notice is the utter silence of this place. Apart from the birds and rustle of branches above, all is tranquil and so quiet.

Why be shy? Let us kiss, there is nobody about, Thomas would whisper as he lay beside you close to the duck pond. And you let him kiss you. You sensed his warm lips on yours and it made you sink into a world you had not known before. A world of sense and sensation. A place where rules changed and were forever changing and changing.

And as you stare over the calm water, you reflect back to a warm day forty years before, when Thomas met you here and stood beside you pointing out towards the center of the pond.

Those are Moorhens, he exclaimed. Look how their heads move.

And you looked and smiled because he had pointed it out to you, something, which you yourself would not have noticed. He turned towards you and caught the excitement in your eyes. And in your eyes I see it all of this, but smaller. As if painted by some miniaturist for some long forgotten noble. He looked away. You sensed his closeness. Something within you wanted him to be closer.

Have you studied much art? You seem to talk so much of artists and art? you asked suddenly. Thomas nodded, but did not turn round.

Only privately, Thomas said, from books and the few galleries I've visited.

Do your parents like art? you asked.

They wouldn't know a Monet from a Matisse, Thomas replied. He was silent for a while and you didn't wish to disturb him further, so kept silent.

A rustle of leaves stirs you back to the present. A blackbird flutters by. You sit down carefully on the grass and place your arms around your legs and lay your chin on your knees, staring at the water. Water does have a calming effect. You close your eyes for a few moments. It isn't until you focus your mind that you realize just how much is going on about you. Sounds of birds; the rustle of leaves and branches; a slight sound of a calm breeze. And you are aware too of your own breathing. And you want at this moment for Thomas to appear beside you. You want his closeness again.You want your youth back. You kiss your naked knees, imaging it is Thomas's lips. You whisper to them words they cannot answer. Where are you Thomas?

Are you at rest? The words are left floating around you. When did I last see him? you ask yourself, kissing your knees again. And you remember roughly the year, not the day, when he passed by with his wife, and his glance at you, and how it seemed to say, I wonder what would have happened between us if I had married you? But he didn't. Then he was gone.

My mother came from Germany, Thomas said. Her parents died in a concentration camp. She was brought over here by an aunt. He was momentarily uneasy. He stared ahead at the water. He turned to look at you and took hold of your right hand. She married my father who was a farm worker in 1947. I don't think it was love. She had lost whatever love she had known. Thomas raised your hand to his lips and kissed it. Then he looked at your hand and turned it this way and then that. Beautiful thing your hand, he said seriously. If I were an artist I'd paint it over and over.

Perhaps you should be an artist, you said, sensing a strange sensation within you.

I've no talent for painting, he exclaimed sadly. I am good at little. I love art and that is it. You and art, now that is something I can equate. And then he kissed you again, but longer that time. It seemed to be an age. And when he released you for breath he had a look about him that made you sense an overwhelming feeling of pity.

As if at any second you would burst out into tears and not know what to say to him. You and art, he repeated softly, you and art.

Do your brothers and sister like art? you asked.

No, Thomas replied bluntly.

Do they like me?

Adore you, Thomas replied, pleased.

Why?

Because you make me happy.

Do I? you replied, surprised.

You know you do.

And how do I make you happy?

In the same way a Monet painting makes me happy.

And how is that? you enquired.

You and it make my life seem more real and meaningful. And when he said those words you felt suddenly opened-up, like a flower. And he kissed you again and again and again.

As you smooth your hand over the grass beside you the memory of its touch punctures you deeply. You feel almost a sharp physical pain in your breast as if someone had stabbed you. You take a quick intake of air and place both your hands down on the grass to steady yourself.

Emily, you worry too much about small things, Thomas said as he sat on the grass and pulled you down beside him. The grass is fine and not damp, he added, seeing your reluctance. He ran his hand over the grass and then lay it against your cheek and you sensed the softness of his hand on your flesh. See, not damp at all.

Thomas what if someone should come? you said, hesitantly sitting beside him.

No one comes here; the place is seldom visited. Thomas held out his hands as if he would banish anything that would appear. He then leaned towards you and brushed his lips against your cheek. Relax, you're a bundle of nerves, he whispered. You feel confused. Part of you feels hesitant, uncertain, the other part wants Thomas closer and to feel his warmth.

Does your mother like me? She seldom speaks to me when she sees me with you, you said to Thomas as he laid his chin on your shoulder.

I think she likes you, Thomas informed unconvincingly. Hard to say with her. She doesn't show her emotions clearly, unless it's hate, then she reveals it as clear as black on white. He rubbed his chin against your shoulder playfully and then kissed your earlobe.

Thomas! that tickles, you said laughing. He does it all the more and you both fall backwards on to the grass. Then he stops and stares down at you as if he were studying a work of art.

Have you ever made love before? he asked.

No, you replied surprised.

Would you, with me? Thomas said, his voice gentle.

When? Not here and now?

But would you at anytime? Thomas asked in his deep voice.

I don't know. I haven't thought about it. And you hadn't. It never dawned on you that he would ask. Yet, deep down, in that darkness, maybe there you might have sensed something. You felt yourself blush as if suddenly you were faced with something like a huge barrier. A forbidden area. You knew little about such matters as your mother never spoke to you about it. You knew what other girls had said at school in the playground during breaks, and that was unconvincing and not helpful. I might, you suddenly said before you could stop the words from leaving. And Thomas smiled as if you'd told him a secret that had been long forbidden.

Looking up at the trees above your head you see the blueness of the sky. The white clouds seem almost too good as if painted by an invisible artist for your benefit. You want Thomas to share this moment with you. You need his presence now to fill in the emptiness within you. And you remember that day a few years back when Thomas's sister stopped you and told you that Thomas had died of cancer. He didn't suffer too much, she had said. And why hadn't I been told? you asked yourself as you stared at her and nodded your head at her words without hearing them anymore. And seeing Thomas as you last saw him you wanted to cry and grab her and shake her and say how much he meant to you, but you didn't, you just nodded and spoke platitudes. Breathing in deeply, you lower your eyes to the water again. You watch as the flies skim over the surface and birds fly over and away to some branch above. Hugging your knees, you want Thomas here with you so much that it is a physical pain him not being there. You lay your lips against your knees and imagine it is him you are kissing. Closing your eyes briefly, you imagine his lips against your cheek. His warm breath against your neck.

Not now, Thomas said, it would be too calculated. Love must be free from calculations and restraints. You were in a sense relieved, but part of you felt let down, as if deflated by a pinprick of reason.

But here? you asked. People might see us.

Serves them right for spying.

I couldn't, Thomas, not here.

Where? Thomas asked spreading his hands outward. Where do you Suggest? You don't know. Thomas's house was out of the question.
His mother was always about spying, searching like an old hen. You think maybe your house, but it would be hazardous, not certain when and if your parents would be in or out.

Here is so open, you moaned. You saw the look in his eyes and the sadness in his face.

Over there, by those bushes, Thomas suggested, pointing behind you. You said nothing, just stared. Then nodded your head slowly.

With your eyes still closed, you sniff the air. It all seems so long ago now. Those days, those inhibitions. That innocence. Fourteen years old then. Just a child in a sense. But something was stirring.

Thomas too was fourteen, but he seemed older, more worldly. Now, it all seems all too much about nothing. Yet, then it was a large gulf to cross. You sigh. Was I really such an innocent? you ask. And deep down inside you know you were. You cannot define innocence to one who is innocent, because once defined they are no longer innocent.

Are you sure? Thomas asked.

Yes.

Now? he asked brushing your cheek with his fingers.

Yes.

Here?

Yes, you replied, looking up at the trees and sky.

You don't mind?

I want to.

Should we? Thomas asked seriously.

Don’t you want to? you asked frowning.

Only without calculation or lust. Thomas uttered softly.

It’s beginning to rain, let’s not, you muttered. But you did, as if the rain was a godsend, a blessing, a purifying of lost innocence. You know now it's all gone. Thomas, innocence, that moment of lovemaking just a metre away somewhere behind you in the bushes.

You open your eyes as if you needed convincing. No Thomas. Just memories that make you happy and sad. Again you sniff the air. You remember Thomas lying there beside you. His hair was wet and his eyes were closed as if asleep.

Was it all right? you asked, shyly.

As good as any Monet, Thomas replied with his eyes still shut.

Are you all right? he asked after a few seconds.

Yes. Strange, as if I have become a butterfly.

Very poetic, Thomas said. It didn't hurt? You didn't reply at first, but sat looking up at the cloudy sky darkening. You did remember a pain, but it was not separate, not a thing a apart; but a part of the process itself, an unfolding of feelings and sensations you had never known before. Thomas sat up and opened his eyes. He stared at you with concern in his eyes. You are all right aren't You? I didn't hurt you?

No, you replied, I’m a butterfly. I'm free. I can fly.

Now you know things better. Your wings are damaged, you can no longer fly. They have been damaged by time and experiences. Soon they will come for you, those in white coats, and take you back and lock you away again. Your freedom will be lost, like your youthful innocence,and dead, not so young, Thomas.

www.ingramcontent.com/pod-product-compliance
Lightning Source LLC
LaVergne TN
LVHW031344150826
845673LV00009B/2850
* 9 7 9 8 6 4 9 1 0 7 9 5 2 *